This book belongs to

....

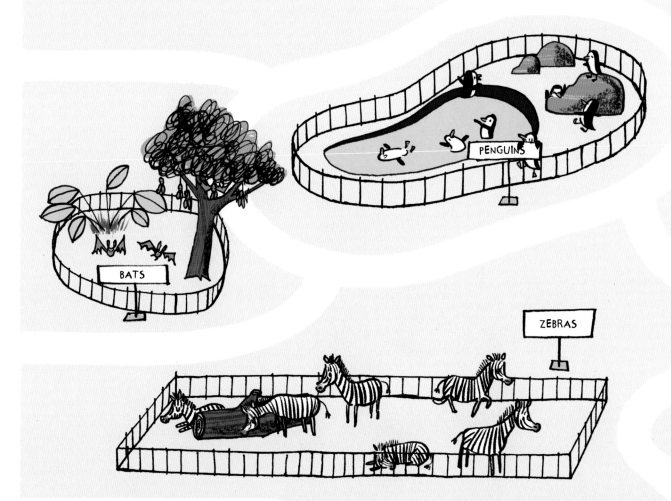

First published 2014 by Parragon Books, Ltd.
Copyright © 2020 Cottage Door Press, LLC
5005 Newport Drive, Rolling Meadows, Illinois 60008

ISBN 978-1-64638-008-4

www.cottagedoorpress.com

I Spy with My Little Eye

ANIMAL ESCAPE

PARROTS

GIBBONS

GIRAFFE

WARTHOGS

FLAMINGOS

cottage door press

Written by Steve Smallman
Illustrated by Nicola Slater

I spy with my little eye something that's white and blue. It's a big, round beach ball! Can you spot it, too?

GAZELLES

ELEPHANT

GIRAFFE

BATS

PARROTS

PENGUINS

TORTOISE

WARTHOGS

ZOO

There's trouble at the zoo today ...

The animals have run away!

Find and follow the tortoise on every page!

GIBBONS

ZEBRAS

FLAMINGOS

TOWN

ZOO

1 very tall giraffe

Spot the little white mouse.

What's that hanging over there? I spy something you can wear. Can you spot the scarf?

trying hard not to laugh.

Where is the ladybug?

Find 1 green bird.

2 elephants in socks

I spy a cat who's fast asleep. I spy a yellow chick. Cheep-cheep!

playing
peek-a-boo
in the
rocks.

Where is the hippo hiding?

Peek-a-boo!

Spot 3 green lizards.

3 orange gazelles jumping high—

Spot the soaring dog—and his hat!

Find my 4 froggy friends.

they don't need trampolines to fly!

I spy with my little eye 5 white bunnies bouncing high. Can you spot them, too?

Spot 2 penguins doing backflips.

4 gibbons, long and slim,

I spy someone hanging around.
Can you find a bat who's upside-down?

Where is my second banana?

Who woke me up?

swinging by the jungle gym!

Spot the balancing lizard.

Who's in there?

Find the jumping mouse.

5 pretty pink flamingos

Spot the pink umbrella.

posing in the bakery windows!

I spy a hippo in a hat. The hat is pink. Do you see that?

Find 4 slithering snakes.

6 zebras, white and black,

Spot the dog in a white hat.

going across the
road and back.

I spy 3 black cats. One, two, three!
How many black cats do you see?

Spot 4 mice out and about.

Where's my other shoe?

7 batty little bats
wearing silly party hats.

Find a boot out of place.

I spy with my little eye a fluttering blue butterfly.
Can you spot it, too?

Where is the little bumblebee?

Spot 10 pink birds
at the party.

Find the thirsty frog.

8 penguins keeping cool

Where is my pink ball?

I spy something extra-sweet. A penguin with a frozen treat!

splashing at the swimming pool.

Spot 2 bunnies in swim caps.

9 sneaky little parrots
hiding by the piles of carrots.

I spy buckteeth and a flat tail.
Can you spot the beaver? (Is he for sale?)

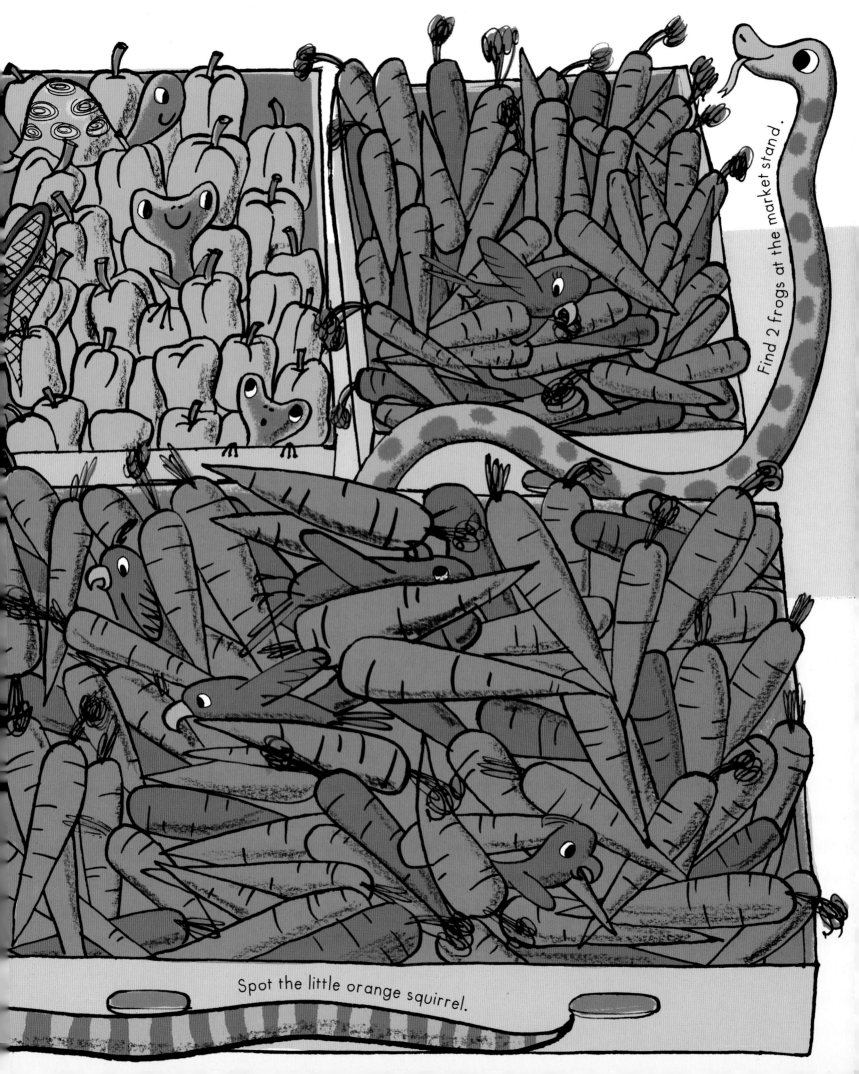

Find 2 frogs at the market stand.

Spot the little orange squirrel.

10 warthogs tapping feet

Spot the snoozing mouse.

Can you find my 2 bunny friends?

I spy someone with brown hair. It's a dancing grizzly bear! Can you spot her, too?

dancing to a hip-hop beat!

Find the fox wearing sunglasses.

Where is my orange bag?

The keeper says,

"Don't make a fuss.
Now, everybody,
on the bus!"

Soon they're back
home in the zoo,

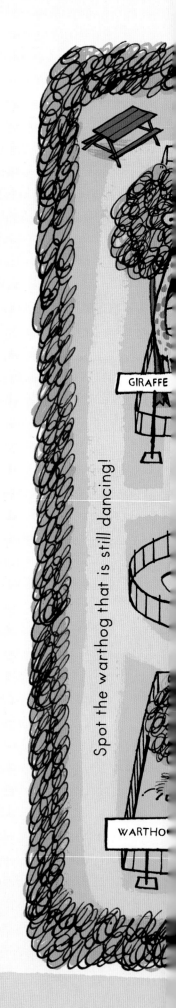

Spot the warthog that is still dancing!

GIRAFFE

WARTHO

but oh no, Tortoise, where are you?

THE END